Little Fox

First published in the UK in 1998 by
Belitha Press Limited, London House,
Great Eastern Wharf, Parkgate Road,
London SW11 4NQ.

ISBN 1 85561 800 1

British Library Cataloguing in Publication Data
for this book is available from the British Library

Printed in Belgium

Editor: Honor Head
Designer: Helen James
Calligraphy: Jan Barger

Little Fox

Jan Barger

Belitha Press

It was supper time, and Little Fox was
being fussy. 'Mouse?' said Mama Fox.

'Yuck!' said Little Fox.

'Worm?' said Mama.

'Yuck!' said Little Fox.

'Chicken?' said Mama.

'Yuck!' said Little Fox.

'Apple?' said Mama.

'Yuck!' said Little Fox.

'Moth?' said Mama.

'Yuck!' said Little Fox.

'Broccoli?' said Mama.

'Yuck!' said Little Fox.

'Mackerel?' said Mama.

'Maybe,' said Little Fox.

'Popcorn?' said Mama.

'Possibly,' said Little Fox.

'Pizza?' said Mama.

'Perfect!' said Little Fox.

'Take away!' said Mama, and they
dashed home for supper.